Cat, Kid and Duck

Written by Charlotte Raby and
Emily Guille-Marrett
Illustrated by James Cottell

Collins

Cat digs a pit.

Kid sits in it.

Cat digs mud up.

Duck in the muck.

Cat kicks a can.

Duck pecks a man.

Kid kicks the mop.

Duck pops on top.

Kid kicks, Duck pecks.

Cat gets set to go.

Cat pops on the mop.

Duck and Kid, no!

14

15

🐾 After reading 🐾

Letters and Sounds: Phase 2

Word count: 50

Focus phonemes: /g/ /o/ /c/ /k/ /e/ /u/ ck

Common exception words: to, the, no, go, and

Curriculum links: Understanding the World: The World

Early learning goals: Understanding: answer "how" and "why" questions about their experiences and in response to stories or events; Reading: children use phonic knowledge to decode regular words and read them aloud accurately, read some common irregular words, demonstrate understanding when talking with others about what they have read

Developing fluency

- Your child may enjoy hearing you read the book.
- Ask your child to read pages 6 to 9, emphasising the rhyming words at the end of each line. You may wish to model this for them first.

Phonic practice

- Look at page 8 together. Model sounding out the word K/i/d and blending the sounds together **Kid**. Explain that this is the name of the goat so it starts with a capital letter.
- Ask your child if they can find another word on page 8 that begins with the letter "k"? (*kicks*) Ask them to sound out the word and then blend the sounds together.
- Look at the "I spy sounds" pages (14–15). Say the sounds together. How many items can your child spot that contain the /c/ sound? (e.g. *kite, kid, cat, cake, king, koala, cup, bucket, cars*)

Extending vocabulary

- Look through the book again together. Ask your child if they can find as many action words as possible. (e.g. *digs, sits, kicks, pecks, pops*)
- Now look at the pairs of rhyming words below. Can your child think of any other words that rhyme with each pair?

    mop   pop   (e.g. *stop, hop, bop, top*)

    get   set   (e.g. *let, bet, met, net*)

    can   man   (e.g. *nan, tan, ban, ran*)